Harold Snipperpot's Best Disaster Ever

To the great Marcelino Poubelle,
the most imaginative problem solver in the world.

Please note:
No animals were harmed during drawing.

Thanks to:
Emmanuel, Sandro, Olimpia my love,
Giancarlo/Gianky, Veronica, Mum and Dad,
Jill, Amy, Béatrice, Paola, Rossella, Jockum and Tomi.

Harold Snipperpot's Best Disaster Ever

words and pictures by

BEATRICE ALEMAGNA

Some days feel like complete disasters. You feel turned upside down, and it seems impossible that anything good could happen.

Well, let me tell you the whole story from the beginning.

It was one week before the disaster, and I was about to turn seven. More than anything, I, Harold Phillip Snipperpot, wanted a real birthday party. I had never had one before because my parents hated parties.

If you want to know why, it's because
they were always very grumpy.

They never hugged or laughed. And forget
about a kiss goodnight – they barely even talked.

So every year on my birthday,
nothing much happened.

But this year I felt extra sad. So sad that my parents got worried. So worried that they decided to do something about it.

'We'll call up Mr Ponzio,' my mum said.

Everyone in our neighbourhood goes to Mr Ponzio with their problems. That's what his job is – to solve people's problems. In very original ways.

'I don't have any kids to send over, but I've got another idea,' Mr Ponzio explained. 'Don't worry one bit, Mrs Snipperpot. We'll throw Harold a party that will be absolutely extraordinary.'

'But will it make our son happy?'

'Yes, of course it will,' he said. 'Trust me! He will never forget it.'

So my parents agreed.

On the day of the party, our house looked great
– all decked out with ribbons, banners, and
a rainbow of balloons. When the doorbell rang,
I ran to answer it.

And wow – we couldn't believe what we saw.

There were real animals,
a long line of them, winding
all the way up the street
to our front door.

We were
flabbergasted.

The animals made their way into our house one by one. At first, everything was fine, and my parents almost seemed to be enjoying themselves.

But before too long, something changed.

The animals began behaving... like animals!

Large mammals, I now know, are born decorators.
They immediately moved the furniture around
and pulled open every drawer.

A polar bear clawed the velvet
sofa while a small herd of sheep
and pigs gobbled up the stuffing
and ate all the cushions.

A giraffe reached up and chomped the crystals right off our Art Deco chandelier – a family heirloom! That was when my father collapsed.

Upstairs in my room, an elephant was taking a nap in my bed and – oh no! – completely squashed my new electric racetrack.

Where was Mr Ponzio? This was a mess!

Meanwhile, a medium-sized flock of birds flew into the kitchen and performed a symphony – on my grandmother's china!

A family of turtles and their reptile friends demolished my father's library and gnawed through an entire shelf of his rare books.

A hippo found her way into the bathroom,
ran a bath, and decided to soak for a while.
All her pond pals followed – overflowing the
tub and flooding the floor! My poor mum.
She was too afraid to look.

Frolicking in my mum's wardrobe were a seal, three monkeys, an armadillo and more, trying on her satin skirts and her silk scarves – and tearing them to shreds. A goat was wearing her shoes!

Our house was destroyed, ruined, turned upside down. Worse yet, it was buried under a carpet of animal poo – of every type – which really stank!

The party was absolutely extraordinary, all right!

Just then, a huge alligator flashed two rows
of sharp teeth at my parents, who, utterly
terrified, jumped into an old steamer trunk.

Oh no! The lid snapped shut
and locked them inside.

I was trying to saw the lid off to
free them when out of nowhere...

...Mr Ponzio appeared, waving a stick!

At the sight of the stick, the elephant panicked and stampeded toward the door. I had just enough time to grab its ears, and the rest of the animals followed us.

There I was, on an elephant, galloping through town, while my parents screamed like crazy from inside the steamer trunk, which was now on top of a rhino! What a drama!

But when I looked around, it all suddenly seemed very funny. Crowds of people gathered in the streets to snap photos of us, adding to the commotion. And it was then that I had the greatest idea.

I, Harold Phillip Snipperpot, took charge and led the entire parade toward the fountain, where each animal stopped and took a sip of water – including the rhino, who dropped the steamer trunk, which fell to the ground and finally opened.

My parents climbed out, looking very relieved, and in front of everyone – I could hardly believe it – gave each other a big kiss. A giant passionate one, just like in a movie.

And then they hugged and kissed me!

Seeing those kisses, the chameleons displayed
their prettiest colours, which reflected in the water
and lit up the entire park. Children from all over
the neighbourhood ran to see.

Some climbed the giraffe's neck, while others sat atop the alligator's back, and others gave the lion a new hairdo.

As for me? My mum swept me up in the air as I laughed and laughed.

Mr Ponzio is our friend now. He's fixed a lot of the broken stuff in my house – even my electric racetrack.

So do you see what I'm trying to say about disasters?
When disasters strike, unbelievable things really can happen.

And if you ask me, goodnight kisses and great new friends are definitely worth a disaster or two.

The End

First published in the United Kingdom in 2019
by Thames & Hudson Ltd, 181A High Holborn,
London WC1V 7QX

This paperback edition first published in 2021

Published by arrangement with HarperCollins *Children's*
Books, a division of HarperCollins Publishers

British Library Cataloguing-in-Publication Data
A catalogue record for this book is available from
the British Library

ISBN 978-0-500-65250-3

Printed and bound in China

Be the first to know about our new releases,
exclusive content and author events by visiting
thamesandhudson.com
thamesandhudsonusa.com
thamesandhudson.com.au